# The Rosie Stories

# The Rosie Stories

by Cynthia Voigt

illustrated by
Cat Bowman Smith

Holiday House / New York

For Walter, Jessica, & Peter,
because it was so much fun
C. V.

To my little Claire
C. B. S.

Text copyright © 2003 by Cynthia Voigt
Illustrations copyright © 2003 by Cat Bowman Smith
The text typeface is Cheltenham.
The artwork was created with gouache.
All Rights Reserved
Printed in the United States of America
www.holidayhouse.com
First Edition

Library of Congress Cataloging-in-Publication Data
Voigt, Cynthia.
The Rosie stories / by Cynthia Voigt; illustrated by Cat Bowman Smith.
p. cm.
Summary: Rosie, a dog who loves to eat, waits for breakfast,
gets into the garbage can for lunch, and joins the family
in following along with an exercise video.
ISBN: 0-8234-1625-9 (hardcover)
[1. Dogs—Fiction.] I. Smith, Cat Bowman, ill. II. Title.

PZ7.V874Go 2003
[E]—dc21
2002191330

# Contents

# Good Morning, Rosie!

In the morning, Rosie had breakfast.

But first Mommy and Jessie and Duff had their breakfast. They sat on the stools to eat.

Rosie waited. They ate. Rosie got up, drank some water, and waited some more. They ate some more. Rosie sat and waited and watched.

In the morning, Rosie had breakfast, but first Daddy made his sandwiches for lunch. Daddy didn't eat breakfast.

Rosie did. She was waiting for breakfast.

"Did you wash your face?" Mommy asked Duff.

"Yes," Duff said.

"Did you wash your face with soap and warm water?" Mommy asked.

"No," Duff said.

In the morning, Rosie had breakfast, but first somebody had to bring down Rosie's bowl. Rosie's bowl was on top of the refrigerator. Rosie went with Daddy to the refrigerator. "Eat!" Rosie barked. "Breakfast!"

"Not yet, Rosie," Daddy said.

"I'm not hungry," Jessie said to Mommy.

Rosie was hungry. She was waiting.

"Finish your juice anyway," Mommy said. "You'll have to wash your face, Duff—and your hands, too—and with soap and warm water."

"I'll do it tonight," Duff said.

"Breakfast!" Rosie barked. "Now!"

Rosie climbed up and put her head on Mommy's leg. "It's not time yet, Rosie," Mommy said. Her hand scratched Rosie's ears. Rosie was

waiting for time and for breakfast. It was nicer to wait when her ears were being scratched.

"Could I wash the car?" Duff asked.

"We should have named Rosie Stomach," Jessie said. "All she wants to do is eat."

"I could wash the car," Duff said, "and you could pay me."

"I think we should have named her Spot," Daddy said. "I always wanted a dog named Spot."

Mommy rubbed Rosie's head, on both sides.

"You could pay me a dollar," Duff said. "Or you could pay me a dollar and a half."

"I always wanted a dog named Fang," Mommy said. "What do you think, Rosie; would you like to be named Fang?"

"Ignore us, Rosie. Your name is just fine," Jessie said. "Besides, we named you." Rosie ran over to let Jessie scratch behind her ears.

"Nobody answered," Duff said. "So I guess you *will* pay me a dollar fifty for washing the car. You didn't say no," he said.

"You need to wash your face before you even think about washing anything else, Duff," Mommy said. "And your hands."

Rosie waited. It was almost time. Rosie sat beside Duff's stool. Her tail wagged because it was almost time for breakfast. In the morning, Rosie had breakfast.

But first, Duff spilled his cereal.

"Uh-oh," Duff said.

Cereal splashed down onto the floor, and milk dripped down onto the floor, and Duff's bowl bounced down onto the floor. The bowl went around and around and around.

Rosie jumped on the bowl.

"Oh, Duff," Mommy said.

"Oh, Duff," Jessie said.

"Oh, Duff," Daddy said. "What about cleaning up this mess?"

"Yo, Rosie," Duff said. "I've got a job for you."

Rosie's job was to eat. Cereal was crunchy and sweet. Milk was silky and sweet.

"Good dog, Rosie," Duff said. "You're doing a good job."

Milk dripped down from the counter. Rosie stood right there, to do her job.

"Mop up Rosie, too," Jessie said. "She's got milk on her head. Why aren't you more careful, Duff?"

"Don't call me that," Duff said. "Don't call me
Duff. My name is Peter." He mopped at the floor
with a paper towel.

"Help!" Rosie barked, and she did. She licked
the towel. She licked Duff's face. He patted her
head with the paper towel.

"My name is Peter," Duff said, "and you always
don't call me Peter. It's not fair. You're never fair."

"You're changing the subject," Mommy said.

"Peter is my name," Duff said.

"Peter!" Rosie barked. "Yes!"

"I'll try," Daddy said. "I'm not sure I can remember, but I'll try."

"I have to wash my face," Peter said.

Now Daddy was mopping the floor. He mopped faster than Peter.

Rosie licked Daddy's face.

"No licking!" Daddy said. "Things are bad enough already down here without adding licking."

"No licking!" Rosie barked. Things weren't bad. It was almost time for breakfast. That was good. Things were good.

In the morning, Rosie had breakfast. But first, Jessie and Daddy and Peter had to go to school.

"Bye, Mom," Jessie said.

Mommy kissed Jessie. "Have a good day," she said.

"I think I'll change my name to Claudia," Jessie said.

"Have a good day, Claudia," Mommy said.

"I think I'll change my name back," Jessie said.

"You're not going to change, are you, Rosie?" Mommy asked.

"Yes!" Rosie barked. "Eat!"

"Oh, dear," Mommy said.

"No licking!" Rosie barked. "Change!"

"Don't you argue with me, too, Rosie," Mommy said.

"See you," Daddy said.

Mommy kissed Daddy. "Have a good day," she said.

"I'll work on it," Daddy said. "Get it?" he asked. "Get the joke?"

"Joke!" Rosie barked. "Eat! Change! No licking! Breakfast!"

Rosie got up and walked around Mommy to sit down on the other side. She wagged her tail.

Peter came downstairs. "See you later, alligator," he said.

Mommy kissed Peter. "You smell nice," she said. "Have a good day, Peter."

"I won't," he said.

In the morning, Rosie had breakfast. But first, she had to wait.

And now, all the waiting was finished. Rosie barked, "I'm hungry! It's time! I'm Rosie!"

"All right," Mommy said. "All right. Don't nag."

"Eat!" Rosie barked. "Nag!" she barked. "Breakfast!"

# Hold the Fort, Rosie!

"Rosie? I'm going to the store," Mommy said. "I won't be long. You hold the fort." She closed the door.

"Wait!" Rosie barked. "I'm Rosie!" She ran into the living room and jumped up onto her chair. Through the window she could see Mommy. "Hello!" she barked. "Hold the fort!"

The car went away.

Rosie went into the kitchen. She smelled something and the something smelled good. She smelled food. Somewhere there was food, somewhere close. Rosie could smell it.

The food smell came out from under the sink, where the doors were open. The food smell came out from the tall thing Rosie's family kept under the sink. Sometimes they put food into the tall thing. Rosie remembered! She remembered where the food was!

Rosie climbed up on the tall thing, and it fell down flat onto the floor. Now she could reach the food.

Some of the food wasn't food, and some of it smelled bad. Rosie pushed the bad food away with her nose.

Rosie was happy. She was so happy, she didn't hear the car come back. She was so happy, she didn't hear anything until Mommy opened the door. Mommy was home!

"Hello!" Rosie barked. She ran to see Mommy. "I'm happy!"

Rosie barked all around Mommy's legs, all the way into the kitchen. "I'm Rosie! Hello!"

There was something lying down on the kitchen floor in front of the sink with its open doors.

"Oh, Rosie," Mommy said. "Oh, Rosie, you didn't."

Rosie sat down in the doorway.

"That makes me angry," Mommy said.

Rosie lay down.

"You're a bad dog," Mommy said. "You're a very

bad dog," Mommy said in her soft, angry voice.

Rosie rolled over on her back. She wagged her tail. She wagged her legs.

"Don't give me that I'm-sorry-I'll-never-do-it-again fake act," Mommy said. "You don't fool me for one minute. I know you'll do it again right away if you get the chance."

Rosie wagged everything she could, as hard as she could.

"I guess I left the doors open, didn't I?" Mommy said. "So it was my mistake and I'll clean up." Mommy opened the back door. "Out, Rosie. Go outside; you heard me. You are evil and wicked and I want you out of the house."

Rosie didn't know *evil* and *wicked*, but she knew *bad* and *out*. *Bad* made Mommy angry. Rosie went outside.

She chased a squirrel, but it ran up the apple tree. "Evil!" Rosie barked. "And wicked! Hello!" she barked.

Rosie sat down beside the tree. She knew how to hold the fort. That bad squirrel didn't dare come back. Rosie held the fort until Mommy called her to come back inside.

Before Mommy went to school, she made a sandwich, because Mommy had lunch. Rosie didn't have lunch. She only had breakfast.

"See you later, Rosie," Mommy said. "Hold the fort."

Rosie ran into the window room and jumped up on her chair. "Hold the fort!" she barked. "Take me! Hello!"

The car went away.

Rosie went back into the kitchen. There was food somewhere, food from Mommy's lunch. She could smell it.

The food smell came from under the sink, but the doors were closed. Rosie knew that if she smelled food and scratched on the doors when the doors were closed, the doors would open when she scratched. Rosie remembered! She remembered how to scratch!

Rosie scratched. The doors opened. The food was inside, in the tall thing. She climbed up on the tall thing again and it fell over again, and

Rosie found the good food to eat. She ate all the good food, and then she chewed on the paper that tasted of good food.

Rosie was happy, and she was sleepy, too. She drank some water and then she ran upstairs to Peter's room. She jumped on the bed and closed her eyes and went to sleep.

Someone called Rosie and it was Daddy! Rosie stood up on Peter's bed. Daddy was home! and Peter was home! and maybe Jessie, too! They were home! "I'm here!" Rosie barked. "I'm Rosie!"

"ROSIE!" Daddy called in his big voice, his big, loud voice. Daddy's big, loud voice was his angry voice.

Rosie lay down on the bed. She didn't want to go downstairs.

"ROSIE!" Daddy called.

Rosie wagged her tail.

"ROSIE!" It was Daddy's biggest, angriest voice. "Come down here this minute, you deadbeat dog. Rosie, COME!"

Rosie knew *come*. As slowly as she could, she jumped down from the bed. As slowly as she could, she went slowly to the stairs. Slowly, she went down one stair, and slowly down the next stair. Halfway down, she stopped. Peter was halfway up.

"Yo, Rosie," Peter said. "You're in trouble now."

Rosie wagged her tail.

"Big trouble, Rosie," Peter said. "Prepare to meet your doom."

Rosie wagged her tail as hard as she could. She didn't know *doom* but she knew Daddy's angry voice.

Daddy came up the stairs. He pulled on her collar. Rosie didn't want to go with Daddy when he pulled her collar, when he was angry, when he was angry at her. She pulled backward.

Daddy pulled Rosie into the kitchen. Rosie pulled backward, all the way into the kitchen. She didn't want to be pulled into the kitchen when Daddy was angry. There was food on the kitchen floor.

"Why are you so bad, Rosie?" Jessie asked.
Jessie was angry, too.

"You're really bad, Rosie," Peter said.

Everybody was angry at Rosie. She wanted to
go outside.

Mommy came home. "Bad dog!" Rosie barked. "Out! I'm Rosie!"

"Did she do it again?" Mommy asked. "But I shut the doors."

"See for yourself," Daddy said. "Look at her. She knows she's been bad."

"You'd think she'd learn," Mommy said.

"She has learned," Daddy said. "But what she's learned is where there's garbage, and how to get it out."

"Yes! Out!"

"We should feed her more, so she won't be hungry," Peter said.

"You're not hungry, are you, Rosie?" Jessie asked. "You're just greedy."

"I am having an idea," Mommy said.

Rosie didn't know *greedy*, and she didn't know *idea*. She just knew *hungry*, and *bad*, and *out*.

The next day, after Mommy ate her sandwich, she looked at Rosie.

"*Are* you hungry?" Mommy asked.

"Hungry!" Rosie barked.

"Dumb question," Mommy said. "You're not hungry. You're greedy, and you're smart, too. But you are not underfed. You get plenty to eat."

"Eat!" Rosie barked.

"No sir, Rosie. No more garbage for you,"
Mommy said. "I've had a brilliant idea." Mommy
was happy. Rosie sat and wagged her tail.

Mommy put a long wooden spoon through the
handles of the door under the sink. "I'm going
now," she said. "You hold the fort, Rosie."

"Hold the fort!" Rosie barked. "Don't go!"

The car went away.

Rosie went back into the kitchen. The kitchen
smelled of food and that food smelled good. Rosie
remembered where the food was!

Rosie scratched and scratched, but the doors
didn't open. She smelled and smelled, and she
could smell food.

It was the wooden spoon. That spoon was in
her way.

Rosie growled. "Bad spoon," she growled. "Very bad spoon."

The spoon didn't move.

"Deadbeat spoon!" Rosie growled. "Evil and wicked!"

Rosie was angry. She was very angry. "I'm angry!" she barked. "I'm Rosie! Come!"

The spoon stayed still. That bad spoon stayed just where it was because it was greedy.

Rosie sat down. She kept her eye on that bad spoon and held the fort.

# Let's Get Some Exercise, Rosie!

Rosie didn't have dinner and she didn't have lunch. She only had breakfast. The family had breakfast, and lunch, and dinner, too. After dinner, Peter carried plates into the kitchen and Rosie helped him.

Sometimes when Peter carried plates, he dropped the plate. Sometimes when he dropped the plate, there was food on it.

Then Rosie would help Peter clean up.

One night while Peter and Rosie were carrying

plates, Mommy said, "I rented Jane Fonda."

Rosie didn't know Jane Fonda.

Jessie did. "But that's exercises," Jessie said.

"I know," Mommy said. "That's why I rented it."

"I hate exercising," Daddy said.

"Did you rent me a movie?" Peter asked.

"Nope," Mommy said. "I rented Jane Fonda because I need to get some exercise."

"You can say that again," Jessie said.

"I need to get some exercise," Mommy said again.

Daddy scratched behind Rosie's ear. Rosie leaned her head as near as she could to his scratching fingers.

"You look fine to me," Daddy said. He stopped scratching.

Rosie pushed at his arm with her nose. "Rosie," Daddy said, "cut it out."

Rosie knew *cut it out*. It meant *no* and it meant

*down*; it meant *go away*. She went to see Mommy.

Mommy got up. "Come on, Rosie. Let's go hear what Jane Fonda has to say."

Rosie didn't know Jane Fonda, but she knew *come* and *go*. She went with Mommy.

Mommy turned on the TV and Rosie jumped up onto her chair. Mommy sat on the sofa.

Jessie came in. "I'll wash the dishes in a little

while," Jessie said. She sat in a chair.

Peter came in and sat beside Mommy. "I finished the table," he said. "Is that Jane Fonda?"

They watched TV. Rosie rested, and waited.

Jane Fonda talked. Her voice was like milk. "You will have one foot on the floor at all times," Jane Fonda said.

"I can do that," Mommy said.

Rosie closed her eyes.

Jane Fonda talked and talked, and then music played. Rosie opened her eyes. Jessie was sitting in a chair, watching TV. Peter was sitting on the sofa, watching TV. Mommy was sitting beside Peter, watching TV.

"Keep breathing," Jane Fonda said. "Don't forget to breathe."

"I can do that, too," Mommy said.

Daddy stood in the doorway. "Why are you all just sitting around?" Daddy asked. "Isn't it an exercise tape?"

Rosie jumped down from her chair.

"Not you, Rosie," Daddy said. "Them."

"Stretch," Jane Fonda said. "Stretch." Her voice was like milk with cereal in it, from Peter's breakfast.

"I can do this," Mommy said.

Mommy got up. Peter got up. They stood in

front of the TV to watch Jane Fonda. Jessie got up and stood with them.

They were going to start doing something! Something was going to happen! When something happened, Rosie was glad. When Rosie was glad, she needed to run. She ran into the dining room; she ran around the table; she ran back to jump up and stand up on her chair and watch the family start to do something.

"Grapevine," Jane Fonda said, "and scissor your arms."

Rosie didn't know *grapevine* and she didn't know *scissor*. Rosie didn't have arms. "Yes!" she barked.

Mommy and Jessie moved sideways across the room, with their arms straight out. Peter moved sideways across the room and bumped into Jessie. Jessie bumped into Mommy.

Rosie jumped down. "I can bump!" she barked. "Bump!"

She bumped into Jessie.

"Look out!" Jessie said.

Rosie bumped into Peter. "Look out!" she barked. She bumped into the sofa. Things were happening!

"Knee up," Jane Fonda said. "Pull down."

Rosie knew *down* and she knew *up*. Up she jumped, then down. "Look out!" she barked, jumping up and down.

"Big arms," Jane Fonda said.

"Arms!" Rosie barked.

They waved their arms in big circles, and Jane Fonda talked in her milky voice.

"Big!" Rosie barked.

When it was Jane Fonda, the family didn't sit still to watch TV. When it was Jane Fonda, things happened. Rosie could talk in a milky voice, too. She lifted her nose up high. "O-woo-wooo-wooo!" she talked.

"Rosie," Mommy said, and she laughed, and she waved her big arms. "What are you doing?"

"Exercises!" Rosie barked. "O-woo-wooo-wooo!" she talked.

Daddy was standing in the doorway and laughing, too.

Everybody liked Rosie when they were all laughing.

"Chicken wings," Jane Fonda said.

Rosie knew *chicken*. Chicken was to eat. Chicken was good.

O-WOO-WOOO

Mommy and Jessie bobbed up and down,
bobbing their elbows up and down.

Peter bobbed up and down, too, bobbing his
elbows up and down.

"Now add a kick," Jane Fonda said.

Rosie didn't know *kick*. She was waiting for the chicken.

Jessie lifted her foot up high.

Rosie jumped up to catch Jessie's foot, but Jessie's foot was already down.

"Kick," Jane Fonda said.

Mommy lifted her foot up high. Rosie was too late to catch Mommy's foot, too. "Kick!" she barked. Mommy lifted her other foot. Rosie jumped.

"Down, Rosie," Mommy said.

"Kick," Jane Fonda said.

Peter lifted his foot up. His foot didn't go as high as Jessie's and Mommy's. Rosie jumped. "Kick!" she barked. "Kick!" And she caught Peter's foot.

Peter thumped down onto the floor.

"Get up!" Rosie barked. She jumped on Peter.
"Kick!"

"Now take it forward," Jane Fonda said.

"Forward!" Rosie barked. "Forward!"

"Get off!" Peter said. "That hurts!"

"I can't take it forward, Jane," Mommy said.

"My dog is in the way. My children are in the way."

"I'm not in your way," Jessie said. "You're in *my* way."

"Forward!" Rosie barked. "Kick!" She jumped at Jessie's foot.

"And my husband is laughing at me," Mommy said.

"I'm not," Daddy said. "I'm laughing at Rosie."

"Laugh!" Rosie barked. "Kick! Forward! Yes! I'm Rosie!"

Peter sat down on the sofa. "I'm tired," he said.

"I'm not," Jessie said. She sat down in a chair.

"This next change is a little complicated," Jane Fonda's milky voice said.

"I quit," Mommy said. She sat down in a chair and watched Jane Fonda on TV. Rosie didn't know what would happen next.

"Are you all stopping?" Daddy asked. "Why are you all stopping?"

"Don't get breathless," Jane Fonda said in her

voice like cereal and sugar and milk on the kitchen floor. "Slow it down if you get breathless."

Rosie didn't know *breathless*. She jumped back up onto her chair. She was happy. She liked exercises. She liked things happening. She liked Jane Fonda and her milky voice.

"O-woo-wooo-wooo," Rosie talked.

"That's right," Jane Fonda said. "That's very good."

ROSIE lived with the Voigts in the city of Annapolis for the first five years of her life. There, whenever she ran from the house, her family had to get into the car to catch up with her and save her from getting into BIG trouble, the kind no dog wants to get into. For the last five years, however, Rosie lived in Maine, where she could run away any time she wanted to. In Maine almost all of the troubles she got into were little ones, like skunks. Rosie preferred living in Maine, even with the skunks.